Princess Truly

I Am Mighty!

WRITTEN BY
Kelly Greenawalt

ART BY
Amariah Rauscher

ACORN™

SCHOLASTIC INC.

For Calista, Kaia, and Ansley—my mighty girls. — KG

For Nika. — AR

Text copyright © 2022 by Kelly Greenawalt
Illustrations copyright © 2022 by Amariah Rauscher

Library of Congress Cataloging-in-Publication Data
Names: Greenawalt, Kelly, author. | Rauscher, Amariah, illustrator.
Title: I am mighty! / by Kelly Greenawalt ; illustrated by Amariah Rauscher.
Description: First edition. | New York : Acorn/Scholastic Inc., 2022. |
Series: Princess Truly ; 6 | Audience: Ages 4-6. | Audience: Grades K-1. |
Summary: In rhyming text, Princess Truly uses her strength and her magical curls to help her friends, rescue her dog from a tire swing, and win a prize at the carnival.
Identifiers: LCCN 2021045108 | ISBN 9781338818826 (paperback) | ISBN 9781338818833 (library binding)
Subjects: LCSH: Princesses—Juvenile fiction. | Superheroes—Juvenile fiction. | Dogs—Juvenile fiction. | Carnivals—Juvenile fiction. | Stories in rhyme. | CYAC: Princesses—Fiction. | Superheroes—Fiction. | Dogs—Fiction. | Carnivals—Fiction. | Stories in rhyme. | LCGFT: Stories in rhyme.
Classification: LCC PZ8.3.G7495 Iai 2022 | DDC [E—dc23
LC record available at https://lccn.loc.gov/2021045108

10 9 8 7 6 5 4 3 2 1   22 23 24 25 26

Printed in China   62

First edition, October 2022

Edited by Rachel Matson
Book design by Sarah Dvojack

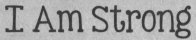
I Am Strong

I am Princess Truly.
I am a mighty girl.

I can do anything.

Watch me jump, flip, and twirl.

I can swing on the bar.
My arms are very strong.

4

Watch me stand on my hands.
I can stay there so long.

My legs are powerful.
I can run up the hill.

6

I want to lift this rock.

I am strong, so I will.

This is my friend Lizzie.
She's a mighty girl, too.

We are both very strong.
Look at what we can do.

We will work as a team.
Mighty girls can have fun.

It is time to play ball.
Watch us hit, catch, and run.

When you're a mighty girl,
you can do lots of stuff.

If you try very hard,
there is nothing too tough.

I Can Do It

squeak!

Sir Noodles wants to play.
I squeak his fluffy bear.

He wants me to throw it.
I toss it in the air.

Now let's go play outside.
We slide across the floor.

I squeak his bear again.
I toss it out the door.

Sir Noodles likes this game.
I throw the bear up high.

He jumps up to catch it,
and flies into the sky.

Oh no! My pug is stuck.
Noodles cannot get free.

I am a mighty girl.
This is a job for me!

I try to push him out,
but the swing spins around.

I try to pull him out.
I lie down on the ground.

Sir Noodles will not budge.
I know just what to do.

I have a good idea.
I need some magic, too.

I tug and then I twist.
My magic curls shine bright.

I know I can do this!
I pull with all my might.

Sir Noodles tumbles out.
Hooray! My pug is free.

I can do anything.
Sir Noodles kisses me.

I Can Win

I love the carnival.
My brother Ty does, too.

We'll have lots of fun here.
There is so much to do.

We pick the tallest ride.

We zoom and then we spin.

We eat cotton candy.

We play games, and we win.

Ty shoots the ball and scores.
He wins a basketball.

I spy a purple cow.
I want that most of all.

35

The game looks very hard.
I want to win this prize.

I must knock down the pins.
I only get three tries.

I toss the beanbag high.

I miss and hit the floor.

It is just my first try.
I'm glad I have two more.

I throw and miss again.
I will not give up now.

I believe in myself.
I'll win that purple cow!

I throw the beanbag hard.

I knock down every pin!

Mighty girls don't give up.
We try hard and we win.

About the Creators

Kelly Greenawalt is the mother of seven amazing kids. She lives in Texas with her family. Princess Truly was inspired by her mighty daughters who can do anything they set their minds to do.

Amariah Rauscher lives near New Orleans with her family. She spends most of her day drawing and painting. In her spare time Amariah can be found lifting weights and hoping to one day be as mighty as Princess Truly.

Read these picture books featuring Princess Truly!

YOU CAN DRAW PRINCESS TRULY!

1 Draw the side of Princess Truly's face. Add her hair.

2 Draw her shirt.

3 Add her arms and her right hand.

4 Draw her tutu and her baseball bat.

5 Add her legs and shoes.

6 Color in your drawing!

WHAT'S YOUR STORY?

Princess Truly feels mighty when she plays ball with her friends.
What is a game that makes **you** feel mighty?
Who do you like to play with?
Write and draw your story!